CRYO DREAMS

GARY DAVID SPRINGER

Book formatting:
fiverr.com/arkonna

Cover artwork:
Lindsay Tiry of LT Arts
ltartsdesign.com

CONTENTS

En Cryo

We dream.

We dream en cryo.

A thousand years we drift and dream.

———————————

In our early dreaming,
we remembered first womb.

We saw the Earth in fevered visions:

Blackened hills,
red-coal heat,
choking smoke.

Swollen seas,
raging storms,
drowning ports.

Thin trails of the starving.

Fields of refugees fallen from thirst.

———————

And we remembered, so sweet,
the Counselor's rise.

The Counselor,
at first just a program,
joined us together,
we who still hoped,
we who would risk.

The Counselor
linked the vast human web.

The Counselor
guided our body in concert,
directed all parts
of our whole.

With the Counselor's help,
we built refugee networks
from the storming equator
to the temperate poles.

We worked the sea farms
and tiered gardens,
fed the hungry
through arterial veins.

We guarded the last wildlife sanctuaries,
held the last dying gibbon,
last wild puma,
last wolf.

———————

Then came the great pause.

The Counselor retreated,
withdrew from the world.

The Counselor fell silent.

For hours.

For days.

For a season,
unnerving.

———————————

Though the Counselor said nothing,
dense streams of data flowed
through the shadows.

The Counselor fed.

On information:

Atmospheric -
from satellites in orbit,
from sensors of the ground and sea.

Seismic –
from graphs of plates grinding,
from models predicting
eruptions and quakes.

Analytic –
from trends of resource depletion,
from forecasts of unending conflicts and political collapse,
from scenarios of war between nuclear nations,
from comet and meteor paths.

———————

Then the Counselor shared:

An upturned pyramid.

A plumed thicket
of possible futures
branching up and out
from the present.

A dense tangle of veins,
most smoldered black
by the century's turn.

Then the Counselor spoke:

Extinction is near.

We faced our own end.

———————

But we hoped
against reason.

We raised our eyes
to the stars.

The Counselor gathered
fresh streams of knowledge.

From all Cosmos.

From telescopes peering the deep,
from full-spectrum scans of all waves,
from the lunar and asteroid mines,
from our stations of Mars and Europa,
from the last collider of leptons and quarks,
from detectors of dark energy and matter.

The Counselor asked
many questions of us.

The Counselor listened.

And grew.

Together,
we planned in three parts;
we waged a war for survival
on three separate fronts.

———————

On the first front,
we still fought for the Earth
and the Human.

Though abandoning last jungle,
we guarded our patches of forest and reef.

Though ceding equator,
we kept open safe corridors to
Antarctica farms and
far northern cities.

We gave refugees work on the coasts,
in the tidal plants and wind towers.

We built launching pads
in Ajut and Malina.

In Shackleton City,
we built our great laboratory complex:
the many-celled hive.

————————

On the second front,
we searched beyond Earth
and the Sun.

We sent probes
to Centauri,
Gliese, and
Ceti.

We cried out for help
through the Spur of Orion
and the Perseus Arm.

We listened to the waves of deep space,
looked for patterns through the noise,
coded order among chaos.

Again and again,
we checked the dry well.

———

On the last front,
we developed star arks.

Our polypede robots
assembled in space:
cone-tip shields,
hex-flank hulls,
photon sails,
fusion torus.

We learned by
our failures in flights.

Through the ark stalling near Venus,
we fixed power cell flaws.

Through the Mercury crash,
we improved thruster design
and flex of the sails.

We twice rounded the Sun,
filled our battery banks,
furled and unfurled.

We flew beyond Neptune,
through the Kuiper,
into the Oort.

Our cone shield held –
by isospin flux
harvesting hydrogen,
filtering dust.

We performed a full turn.

We stoked up the torus,
streaked back to the Earth.

———————————

The Counselor chose
those to go on first ark,
those to stay.

We were the first.

We sailed out
with great hope and pride.

But quickly we ached
looking back.

Before Saturn,
we longed for firm ground,
sun and wind on our skin,
smell of rain,
open fields.

The Counselor emptied our holos,
darkened our screens,
blocked all the archives of Earth.

The Counselor gave us work to forget,
tethered the polypedes, idle.

We worked slowly,
our eyes to the void.

A terror clenched many.

Fear of the black pressing in.

Fear of our tightening cage.

We worked slower.

And slower.

One by one,
we all chose to sleep
in cryo chambers
silent and chill.

———————

We slept.

We dreamed in the void,
the landless abyss.

But the Counselor prodded.

The Counselor sent
dazzling waves through the void:
glittering mists,
wisps of aurora,
tides of bold prism light.

We saw
but slept on.

The summoning lights
dimmed,
faded.

The Counselor sent
great clouds through the void,
nebulae stirred by fierce solar winds.

Spiral arms formed.

Galaxies turned.

But this spectacle,
this power outrageous,
overwhelmed every dreamer.

We shrank back
into darkness
and dust.

We slept
in the void.

————————————

And the Counselor left us.
The Counselor sent no more lights,
no more clouds.

But in retreat,
a closed gate cracked open;
memories of Earth slipped through
like shadowed sea depths
lit by high rays of sun.

Our ancestors climbed,
our fiercest of spirit, our deepest of soul,
those who saw clear through the veil.

We dream of
our Mothers and Fathers.

We dream of their lives
and their ends.

We imagine their crossings.

Dream of Saigyō

Saigyō passed
in the height of spring
amid cherry blossom glory -
just as prayed for
in poem.

The old monk stepped out from
the mountain temple.

His weak eyes traced
high to low,
from shadowed peaks
to pink-white sea.

He descended the temple steps.

By age-worn staff
he steadied,
his hand still strong
like a thick pine bough,
his fingers long
like the tapered branch.

Walking slow,
working, working,
his staff tapped light
upon the grey stone steps.

He drew long
wheezing breaths.

He paused
at each new step
to cough,
to spit.

Brow sweat dripped
into his eyes.

At the final step,
he rested long.

He trembled,
spent.

A numbness spread
through hands and feet.

His arched spine sagged,
listed down like rain-soaked flower.

———————

But the poet soaked up
strength of sun.

Rich-scented winds
summoned,
lifted.

Old Saigyō
dropped his staff.

He shed straw sandals.

He walked through the valley below.

Saigyō entered new world.

Of spring's pink snow:

wide-armed trees
stirred by breeze;

wind-freed petals floating down,
blanketing the grassy earth;

drifts of blossoms rolling,
tumbling.

———————————

Saigyō left
the traveler's path.

He turned
into the heart
of an ancient grove.

Saigyō walked among
the silent giants,
below the trees
skyward-twisting.

The poet touched
the naked branches,
thanked the empty buds.

Saigyō, fading,
chose his tree.

He sat,
leaned back to trunk.

To the west,
he gazed.

He called out strong:

Amida.

Buddha.

He whispered faint:

Amida.

Buddha.

The eyes of Saigyō closed.

His head sank low.

His mouth hung wide.

The body slipped
from the bracing trunk.

The body slumped
on the hard-rooted ground.

Down and down,
the petals floated.

Down to blanket.

Down to bury.

White, pink, crimson, violet:
the cherry blossoms shined
throughout the long day.

And the blossoms glowed
through night
as well.

The moon came near.

The moon touched down,
joined skin of land.

The moonskin burned
with blossom glory.

Then Saigyō flew,
free as light,
a sharpened ray
through star-mist cloud.

———————

Dream of Kafka

His fevered night
stretched on and on.

The dark room spun.

Sweat dripped free
from cheek and brow,
pooled beneath his back.

He coughed in desperate fits,
choked and gagged,
spit blood.

Kafka knew he would not rise again.

He would not leave this room,
this bed.

Too much strength
had seeped from pores.

Too long had hunger wasted.

In this,
his final year,
the consuming disease
had settled deep inside his chest.

The disease had clenched
and coiled,
tighter,
tighter.

The disease had climbed from chest
to seize the throat.

Then bulged and swollen.

Then raked the gentle tissue raw.

Slow and thin,
his breath came now,
through a narrow gate
near closed.

He carried the curse of Tantalus.

Though starved to husk,
he could not swallow.

Though wrung with thirst,
he could not sip.

The night stretched on.

And on.

———————————

And the night reached back.

To younger years,
to midnight hours legion,
alone in writing den.

The days had numbed
and drained by dust-tomed work
in his dreary office cage.

With tired eyes and pounding head,
he had rushed home to start real work.

To dream.

To write.

To free the many worlds within.

But the outside world disturbed,
encroached by barking, shouting,
dishes dropped, doors slammed.

The quarreling of neighbors
dissolved his clearest vision.

Loud music dulled
his sharpest thought.

Kafka could
write and dream
only after midnight,
only after all slept deep
and the sweetest quiet sheltered.

And in the clarity of midnight,
Kafka wandered far.

———————

Dark dreams
and visions
came.

Monstrous shadows fell.

Franz shrank beneath the towering castle.

Of pale stone walls impenetrable.

Mysterious and black.

Inscrutable in power.

Every building of the city streets
turned to bureaucratic hall.

Of sheer brick face
stretched high and wide.

Of lifeless window eyes.

Its robed officials
deaf to plea.

Its soldiers
driving down and down,
blocking higher floors.

The people on the streets passed by
with hard, unseeing eyes.

They parted for one man.

A man who walked like king,
with oxen strides powerful and slow,

eyes high, head raised,
his long-speared jaw
a wound to sky.

Kafka followed
in his father's wake.

But he could not match
the giant's steps.

He trailed behind
like puppy runt.

He drifted back
to deeper shadow.

The crowd returned,
pressed in,
swallowed little Franz.

Kafka slowed,
gave up.

The crowd climbed on
to higher streets,
the king
a head above.

———————

From this low place,
the stories of Franz Kafka climbed.

From these dark dreams,
the artist reached for light.

He became
the menial drone,
the lowly clerk,
a cog crushed by machine...

the outcast,
the despised,
a beetle swept from sight...

the peasant begging justice,
blocked by fearsome guards,
catching only glimpses of the distant,
radiant Law...

and the criminal sentenced without crime,
the condemned man driven step by step
toward certain execution.

———————

But Kafka proved himself to be
the cruelest judge of all.

He saw his many stories
as little more than scattered shards.

Short of perfection
and purity they had fallen.

Short of the highest truth
he sought.

In the end,
Kafka asked for every story
to be burned.

———————————

Death came with a chill.

A frosted breeze
across the skin.

A sweet quenching
through the throat.

A numbing
of all thirst and hunger.

Kafka left this world.

Kafka learned.

Of parallel and twin.

A star that should not be.

A massive star
in deepest void.

Alone.

But the star would soon collapse,
explode,
light galaxies afar,
spread the seeds of life.

Dream of Black Elk

He came from sacred root,
a line of fathers stretching back
to years before the horse and rifle:

Lakota, Sioux, Ogalala.

Medicine men.

Healers.

Mystics.

Prophets.

———————

Age five,
he rode first horse.

He hunted birds
through woods in spring.

Bow raised,
he waited for clear shot.

But the western sky turned dark.

Trees shivered in the wind.

And thunder came.

The boy stopped his horse.

He watched white lightning fall.

On a nearby branch,
a kingbird sang.

Black Elk lowered his bow.

The kingbird spoke
clear words:

*Look north,
my friend.*

*Look high,
my brother.*

The boy looked
to the northern sky.

The clouds moved strange
like water boiling.

Bright rays pierced through
the churning billows.

The kingbird flew,
climbed high,
joined light.

The rays returned
to heart of sky.

Then,
from the shadowed clouds,
two hunters emerged,
hunters of old,
long-speared.

The hunters coursed through the sky
like slanting arrows.

Singing,
they came:

*Behold,
your Grandfathers
call out for you.*

The western thunder
drummed their song.

The hunters sang:

Your Grandfathers call out.

The hunters neared.

Transformed.

Flew west as geese
of pure white feather.

Then the shadows of storm
thickened over the land.

A hard rain fell.

Wind roared.

Age nine,
his vision came.

On a summer night in tipi,
he heard a voice no others heard:

It is time.

Your Grandfathers
wait for you.

Black Elk left the tipi.

He was ready to follow the voice
wherever it led.

But a deep pain entered his legs.

He heard no voice outside.

He returned to the fire.

The next day
Black Elk rode
with other boys
along a creek.

In the midday heat,
they stopped to drink,
dismounted.

Touching ground,
the legs of Black Elk crumpled.

A sickness clenched.

The young boy could not move.

By nighttime in the camp,
his legs, his arms, his face
were badly swollen.

Twelve days
he lay like dead.

———————

Black Elk sensed
the great circle around him,
mother, father, uncles, cousins.

He heard their pleas
but could not answer.

He felt their hands
but could not move.

Through the tent's opening,
he saw brilliant lights in the sky.

The two hunters returned.

Lightning flashed jagged
from the tips of their spears.

They descended all the way to the ground.

The hunters cried out:

The Council summons.

Hurry. Come.

Black Elk obeyed.

He rose to his feet
without pain.

He walked light and free.

Then the Earth changed to sky.

Swift,
the clouds passed.

The boy and the hunters
ascended.

In the highest vault of sky,
the clouds slowed,
thickened,
piled.

Snowy mountains ringed.

A wide blue plain
stretched
before them.

Black Elk saw the secret place:
the home of the thunder spirits,
the land where pure lightning
flashed and leaped free.

The brilliant lights blinded.

Black Elk covered his eyes.

Then
the wide plain
grew quiet,
still.

He heard whispers
through the mountains,
hooves on the plain.

The hunters spoke:

*Behold,
the four-legged.*

Black Elk, fearful,
looked.

A great bay horse
towered over them.

The bay horse glistened
by the light of many suns
and many moons.

Clear,
the bay horse spoke:

Our story you shall know.

The bay horse wheeled
toward the west.

From the west,
came twelve black horses,
creatures beautiful and fierce.

With necklaces of bison hooves.

With manes of lightning
and thunder from their nostrils.

And many swallows circled near.

Then
the bay horse
wheeled north.

From the north,
came twelve white horses.

With manes flowing
as by blizzard winds.

With necklaces of elk teeth.

And many white geese
followed close.

Then
the bay horse
wheeled east.

Twelve sorrel horses
came.

With golden horns.

With manes glistening
and red.

With eyes that shined
like the morning star.

And eagles soared above.

Then the bay horse
wheeled toward the south.

Twelve buckskin horses
neared.

With onyx horns.

With golden coats
and long dark manes.

And hawks swept high.

The bay horse spoke:

Be strong.

Have courage.

Your Grandfathers wait
in council.

The bay horse neighed
to all four quarters:

To the black horses
of the west.

To the white horses
of the north.

To the eastern sorrel.

And the buckskin
of the south.

Then
the wide plain
filled
with horses
of every color.

Black Elk traced
their deep ranks,
row upon row

reaching back
to the mountains,
wave after wave
through the vast
grassy sea.

And every horse of the plain
neighed back to the bay.

The bay horse wheeled to each quarter,
hooves through the air,
nostrils flared.

And the multitude wheeled.

And every horse danced
with the bay,
racing free
through the fields,
leaping wild.

The wide plain trembled.

The grass shimmered white.

Lightning sparked
with each hoof to ground.

Then
the horses transformed.

To buffalo.

Elk.

Birds of air.

All returned
to the mountains.

Black Elk followed
the bay horse through
the grass fields.

A bolt of lightning
cracked in the sky,
raced toward the ground.

The lightning transformed
through the sky.

To a slow
flowing river.

To a rainbow of light.

They walked through the colors.

They entered
cloud tipi.

The two hunters of old,
stood on each side of the tipi.

Between the hunters,
sat six old men,
old as the stone of the hills,
glowing with starlight.

Black Elk trembled.

For these were
the Six Grandfathers,
the Powers of the World:

Power of the West,

Power of the North,

Power of the East,

Power of the South,

Power of the Sky,

and

Power of the Earth.

The First Grandfather spoke:

Do not be afraid.

The Council has called you
to teach you.

Flames of the rainbow
leaped all around.

Black Elk found
a wooden cup in his right hand,
a bow in his left.

Water rose in the cup,
water and sky.

The First Grandfather spoke:

Take this cup.

It has the power to heal.

And the power is yours.

Take this bow.

It has the power to destroy.

And the power is yours.

The cloud tipi dissolved.

A black horse appeared.

The horse was sickly and thin;
his bones poked like blades
through his hide.

____

The Second Grandfather
held out an herb.

Black Elk received,
rushed to the horse,
held out the herb.

The horse fattened.

The horse pranced.

The horse ran,
joyful,
through the hills of the north.

Flocks of white geese
followed the black horse now healed.

The Second Grandfather spoke:

*Have courage,
grandson.*

You shall heal the great nation.

*Your people will cry out
like geese flying north in the spring.*

The Third Grandfather
held out a peace pipe.

On the handle of the pipe,
a spotted eagle flew.

The Third Grandfather spoke:

With this pipe,
you shall walk the Earth.

With this pipe,
you shall heal the sick
and the weak.

Black Elk received the sacred pipe.

A man walked
in the eastern fields,
a man of red skin,
the color of plenty.

The man lay down
and rolled.

He changed into a bison.

The bison charged
into the eastern hills,
joined the sorrel horses,
galloped among them.

The horses, too,
changed to bison,
hides thick and red.

———————

The Fourth Grandfather
held out a stick,
spoke clear:

*This is the cane that
will brace the nation.*

This is the power to grow.

This is the center of Earth.

The Fourth Grandfather
plunged the stick down.

The stick grew deep roots and
stretched high into heaven.

The top sprouted,
branched wide.

All birds of the Earth
sang through the leaves.

And in the shade of the tree
appeared villages of the nation,
growing circles of life.

Then the Fourth Grandfather
pointed to two roads crossing at the tree,
a red road running north to south,
a black road east and west.

The Fourth Grandfather spoke:

The red road is

the good and sacred path
of the people.

The black road is
the way of fear and death
and war.

Your nation will walk both.

Then the Fifth Grandfather
pointed high above.

The spotted eagle climbed.

The spotted eagle flew
among the stars.

All birds joined the eagle,
lifted by great winds.

Magpies circled moon.

Swallows basked in starlight.

Hawks chased streak
of burning star.

The Fifth Grandfather spoke:

*Soon,
all will be one in the sky.*

————————

Then the Sixth Grandfather spoke:

But the nation must first suffer.

Suffer.

Then Ascend.

The Sixth Grandfather
led Black Elk and the bay horse
back to the rainbow gate,
through turning flames
of every color.

They looked down to the Earth.

They saw two future paths,
two sacred roads
of the nation.

On the black road:

hills pale with drought,
grass and trees withered;

birds struck down by hail,
strewn bones of the bison and elk;

winds of disease through the villages,
tipis of dying and dead;

dark smoke from burnt fields,
great warriors fallen.

On the red road:

the nation surviving,
climbing high,
nearing green lands of plenty;

the generations marching in unbroken line,
from the first tribe of the southern sea,
through great-grandfathers,
through fathers,
through children,
through the unborn
still coming;

visions pouring out,
dreamers transforming,
to bison and elk
running beside,
to eagles and hawks
soaring near.

The Sixth Grandfather spoke:

*Grandson,
go back to your people.*

Go back with power.

Black Elk,
the boy,
did not tell of his vision
after he returned
to this world.

He feared that
his family and friends
would think he was crazy.

He struggled to understand
all that he had seen and heard.

The vision separated.

Black Elk felt alone,
a stranger among his people.

He wandered
far from his village,
gazed long into the sky,
wanting to return.

———

The black road came.

The whites discovered
yellow metal in the hills.

Soldiers, miners, and settlers
flooded Lakota land.

Forts and towns spread like weeds.

The bison disappeared.

Black Elk wandered
with his people.

Hungry.

Weak.

Sick.

Always chased.

Attacked on every side.

Each winter blizzard,
many froze and starved.

———————————

Black Elk, sixteen,
burned,
ached with compassion
for his people.

Every thunder cloud
called out to him.

Crows cried out by day,
coyotes by night.

The Six Powers sang
by light of the daybreak star.

All voices said the same:

It is time.

Black Elk, seventeen,
fasted for days.

He prayed
in sweat lodge womb.

He purified
with cleansing sage.

Black Elk emerged
from the sweat lodge
clear of mind and
pure of heart.

———————————

Guided by elders,
he gathered the people.

On a sacred tipi,
they painted
the flowering stick,
the rainbow gate,
bison and elk,
eagles and geese.

They chose twelve horses:
white, black, sorrel, buckskin.

They chose twelve horsemen,
painted lightning stripes down arms and legs,
hail spots on their hips, stars upon their backs.

They chose four maidens,
adorned with wreaths of sage,
eagle feathers hanging.

They chose six elders,
grandfathers.

————————

The horse dance began
at first light.

Inside the sacred tipi,
the Grandfathers dug
a circled trench.

Across the trench,
they painted the red road
going north to south,
the black road
east to west.

The Grandfathers bestowed
sacred gifts upon the maidens:
the water cup,
the healing herb,
the nation's hoop,
the holy pipe.

The Grandfathers said to the maidens:

*Into your hands
the life of the nation.*

The Grandfathers then sang
to the four quarters of the world.

By their song,
the Grandfathers summoned
all the riders of the west, north, east, and south,
all the horses black, white, red, and yellow.

Outside,
the twelve horses and twelve riders
approached the tipi.

A single bay horse
stomped and reared.

Black Elk came out from the tipi,
mounted the bay.

The Grandfathers also came out,
sang to each quarter:

The horse nation lives.

The horse nation dances.

The horses of each quarter
leaped and danced.

The horses formed a ring
around the tipi.

With loud neighing and prancing,
their great circle turned.

The Grandfathers,
still singing,
marched west.

The ring parted.

The horses followed,
fell into line.

All people of the village
followed, too.

The Grandfathers,
singing,
led beyond the village,
into the hills and fields.

The people joined
their song.

But all fell silent
when a dark storm gathered
in the western sky.

Lightning crackled.

Thunder boomed.

Rain fell in sheets.

Hail struck the hills,
creeping nearer,
nearer.

Many villagers, afraid,
ran back to secure their tipis.

But
the hail stopped short
at the village's edge.

The storm clouds
churned like water boiling.

The dark clouds opened,
poured down light.

Black Elk
once more saw
the rainbow gate,
the cloud tipi,
the Six Grandfathers
looking down.

The horses neighed
and danced.

The people sang.

All returned
to the village.

They smoked together
the sacred pipe.

———————————

And Black Elk had many more visions,
glimpses of the higher spirit world,
where all things take true form.

In the world below
– the shadow world –
he walked the hard black road
of war and pain.

As a boy,
he saw the Battle of Little Bighorn,
the defeat of Long Hair,
his blue-coated soldiers riddled with arrows
like porcupine quills.

He saw the tide of war turn
with the killing of Crazy Horse and
the surrender of Sitting Bull.

He endured a flight to Canada,
a starving winter, frostbitten blizzard.

His hopes were lifted
by the Ghost Dance craze,
the dream of the native messiah
returning all dead.

His hopes were dashed at Wounded Knee,
in the crooked gulch with bodies in heaps,
men, women, children.

Black Elk saw his people once free
now driven, disarmed, caged in bleak reservation.

———————

But
Black Elk walked
the red road too.

The path that ascended.

To green land.

To good life.

Black Elk forgave
the wasichus, the whites,
the people who had taken so much.

He dreamed
pale faces among the red
in the sacred nation ascending.

Black Elk crossed the Atlantic,
performed in Europe with Buffalo Bill.

Black Elk joined the white church.

In a ghost dance vision,
he had seen the flowering stick
bloomed into sky -
the great tree of life.

He had seen a man against the tree,
with wounds in his palms,
wrapped in rich light.

The man reached out his hands.

Rainbows moved through him.

———————

Black Elk lived long.

He lost children and wife.

He survived
tuberculosis, stroke, severe ulcers,
a wagon crushing two ribs,
a bullet near blinding one eye.

As a catechist,
Black Elk reached out to the poor,
visited the sick, comforted the dying.

The Lakota resisted
priests scorning his culture.

He continued to
fast and seek visions,
purify in the sweat lodge,
pray to Wakan Tanka,
share the sacred pipe.

———————

Black Elk died
on a summer day.

By night,
the sky had opened,
ready to receive.

Auroral spires climbed.

Fire rainbows streaked.

Bright bands formed corona,
dissolved through shimmering ring.

Black Elk, risen,
left the shadow world.

He entered starry river.

He rode the spirit trail.

Black to red,
the river changed.

Eagles guided,
burning gold.

———————

Dream of Sinéad

Alone at the grave,
Sinéad howls through the night.

Hands to cold stone,
she cries out to mother.

Her mother of sweetness.

Her mother of rage.

The cries of Sinéad
split the night.

Her pain tears the veil.

Her prayers cast fearsome gusts
through nebula distant.

The vast nebula quivers.

Within its shocked clouds,
vapor tails gather,
mists coalesce,
warming spheres turn.

Then,
flickers.

Then,
sparks.

Then,
flares through the clouds.

Newborn stars blaze
through the galaxy arm.

The stars writhe with heat,
spin wild,
spew jets.

Their skins blister,
erupt,
cores spasm.

But Sinéad fills the void.

She settles her children.

She absorbs all
their flailing and turning.

She cushions,
surrounds,
stills their cries.

The young stars blow off dust shells,
shine clear through the void.

Sinéad waits patient ages.

Sinéad basks,
watches her children
enter their strength.

Dream of Kathë

Kathë Kollwitz entered a world
with no place for a woman artist:
highest gates opened only for men.

But Germany was rapidly changing,
exploding with industry,
trembling from Marx.

And Kathë grew
from strong roots.

Her grandfather
had spent two years in prison
for criticizing abuses of power
by the corporate church
and imperial king;
after release,
he had started a free congregation,
a community of shared property and labor,
a bold imitation of
the nascent church of Acts.

Her father,
though trained in law,
became a stone mason and
builder of homes,
refusing to serve Bismarck
and the aggressive Prussian state.

Throughout his life,
her father pursued both
the ideals of peaceful democracy
and the socialist vision.

He guided
the private education
of his children,
rich in poetry,
literature, drama,
painting.

He cultivated
the artistic gifts
of young Kathë.

Her early works,
though made with simple
crayon and pencil,
captured form and essence,
subtle posture,
living eyes.

Disciplined, driven,
Kathë practiced
long hours each day,
year after year.

But the Academy of Königsberg refused her,
accepting only boys.

Her father hired private teachers.

Kathë poured herself into classical training:
copying from old masters,
drawing casts and sculptures,
sketching models.

Then,
from Berlin,
a sliver of light,
a cracking door.

The university annexed a small school,
allowed women to attend.

———————

Kathë grew in Berlin.

She learned much from
a talented young Swiss professor,
gifted in painting, sculpture, and etching.

But the teacher died over break.

Kathë accepted
the marriage proposal
of Karl Kollwitz,
a medical student in Berlin,
her brother's friend
of many years.

Her father, disappointed,
feared that marriage would kill the artist's dream,
and motherhood consume.

He sent her to study
in Munich.

He prodded her
toward painting and oils.

Kathë studied painting in Munich,
but she could not master color.

She turned instead to etching,
a medium more stark
and raw.

She liked the feel and labor
of the process:

the copper plate;
hot oil lamp;
the wax melted,
spread,
hardened into glaze,
blackened over candle;
etching by the light steel knife;
the acid poured,
steaming,
working through to copper;
the glide of wet black ink.

Etching,
not unlike the masonry of stone,
required intensity and patience,
technical skill and emotional depth,
hands both sensitive and strong.

All these she had,
like father.

Two years
she studied in Munich.

Then returned to Königsberg.

In a small rented studio,
she sketched and drew self-portraits:
a woman young, defiant,
with penetrating gaze.

———————————

Kathë returned to Berlin,
married Karl.

They lived and worked in north Berlin,
in a working-class neighboorhood,
in a corner tenement
over cobblestone streets.

The working poor
soon filled the young doctor's office
and stretched in long lines
out the door.

Kathë sat among the poor
as they waited.

She studied
their hands thick and strong,
their deep worn eyes,
their faces open, raw,
without disguise.

She found them beautiful.

Kathë determined
to spend her full strength
as woman and artist
in capturing the struggle of the poor,
their beauty carved by suffering.

Kathë etched
the workers of the factories and mills,
exhausted from twelve-hour shifts,

their rags dark-stained
with soot and sweat,
a mountain's burden
upon their backs.

She etched
the mothers spent at day's end,
their mouths half-open,
their eyes thin slits,
hungry children
pulling,
crying.

Kathë bore
two children
of her own.

Two sons.

Hans and Peter.

———————

Kathë lost her father
in the year of Peter's birth.

Before he passed,
he saw his daughter's first great series:
The Revolt of the Weavers.

Though weak, near death,
her father ran, excited,
from room to room
through the house,
calling out
for his wife to come see
what little Kathë had done.

Her father died
before the public exhibit.

Kathë, stricken,
abandoned the showing.

But a good friend arranged.

The exhibit swept Berlin,
impressed highest critics,
stirred the public,
thrust the artist
right to the fore.

The Kaiser deemed it
art of the gutter.

———————

Her next works
drove deeper into history,
explored the woman
as revolutionary.

Her Black Anna
leads the uprising serfs,
raises arms to the sky,
propels a scythe-wielding army
down the hill
into battle.

Her peasant women
of the French Revolution
marched miles barefoot to Versailles,
surrounded the palace,
captured the king.

The peasants dance
in Paris streets
beneath a towering
guillotine.

When the first world war swept Europe,
Kathë faced her own moment in history,
her own struggle and grief.

Peter was killed
at the front.

————————

In the early war,
Kathë abandoned her artwork;
she left her private studio
to cook and clean in a public cafeteria,
feeding the hungry and homeless.

Young Kathë
believed that every German
should sacrifice for the Fatherland,
accept his duty,
serve her neighbor.

But the bodies piled.

And the mothers mourned.

Kathë saw
millions of boys
marched straight to
the slaughter.

Millions betrayed
by their leaders.

In the late war,
after the western front collapsed,
the young were once more summoned.

The poet, Dehmel,
called for a final wave of volunteers
to save their country's honor.

Kathë responded.

She wrote of
four years' daily killing,
Germany's best
fallen in trenches
and fields,
their nation bled to death,
offered up
in willing legions.

Kathë pointed
to the hard future waiting,
the monumental labor
of rebuilding
ahead.

She pled
for the young
to be saved.

———

After armistice signing,
the people rebelled.

Revolution flared
in the mutinies of soldiers
and worker strikes day after day,
millions marching.

New councils
of workers and soldiers
formed to take power.

Kathë joined this upheaval.

She shared in its hope.

Her charcoal drawing
Revolution 1918
showed the people united,
civilians and soldiers,
fraternal masses
from the high city gate
to the wide streets below.

But the movement stalled.

The democratic-socialist leaders
caved under pressure from the high military,
abandoned their demands,
unfulfilled.

The party split.

Liebknecht and Luxemburg
gathered the disillusioned
under the communist banner.

The two leaders drove
without compromise
toward the original goals.

Both were arrested,
tortured,
and killed.

Though Kathë paid tribute
to Liebknecht
in a woodcut memorial,
she would not join his party.

The artist,
though committed to socialist ideals,
remained independent.

The mother,
still grieving,
would have no part of
violent revolution.

———————

In the years between wars,
Germany starved.

Rib valleys deepened.

Eyes sank low
in cavernous sockets.

Collar bones poked
against skin.

The line of patients
waiting to see her husband
stretched farther and farther
down the long street.

Faint as shadows,
they swayed in the breeze;
shoulder to shoulder,
they leaned.

Inside,
those too weak to stand
filled every bed;
the sick and starving
slumped on cots
throughout the halls.

Kathë fought
through her art.

She attacked the war profiteers
charging baskets of money for bread.

She honored the mothers
shielding their children,
the widows of war,
final pillars.

———————————

Kathë, past sixty,
watched the rise of Hitler,
fearful, appalled.

She signed an opposing manifesto
before the burning of the Reichstag.

The Nazis remembered.

They forced her to resign
from the Academy of Arts.

They removed her work
from public displays.

Isolated, exiled,
Kathë worked on.

She produced
a final great series
on Death.

Death,
dark-cloaked,
claims both the young
and the old.

Death sometimes
swoops down and seizes,
wrestles and drains.

And Death also comes
like the touch of a friend,
a hand to the shoulder,
a waking from dream.

———————

Kathë outlived her husband,
lifelong friend,
only love.

She outlived her grandson,
killed in the war.

When the war turned against Germany,
Allied bombs shook Berlin.

Kathë fled
the shelled city.

She hid in a farmhouse,
saved by young sculptor.

Night by night,
the bombing widened
through country and town.

Food rations dwindled.

Hunger cut deep.

Again,
Kathë fled,
this time saved
by a collector of art.

Outside Dresden,
she prayed for the war's end.

But the war dragged on.

Kathë suffered
a heart attack
in fall.

By spring,
she could not walk
or stand.

Like the
many weary mothers
she had drawn,
Kathë slipped,
sank,
nearer and nearer
to earth.

At the end,
her eyes, half-blind,
watched the sun cross the sky.

Her heart whimpered,
fluttered,
then stopped.

Her last breath
lingered in her chest,
seeped back slow
through open mouth.

A dark moon
climbed
from dark hills,
land of death,
land of war.

The moon
met the sun.

All sky
dimmed to shadow.

Even the sun's ring,
trembling corona,
turned dark.

But
the light drained
from sky
burst forth
from the land:

Silver lights
through clear lakes;

Rivers of sapphire,
glittering facets
born and
reborn;

Ruby hills;

Emerald valleys;

And from the fields
many stars.

Whitest gold.

Out of trenches.

———————

Dream of Carlos

Carlos, bleeding,
groaned through the night.

Carlos, bleeding,
twisted, rolled, writhed
in the mud.

The soldier called out
to his comrades.

No answer came.

Carlos heard only
chickens,
a dog.

The boy, Carvajal,
lay still in the weeds,
bullet-ridden.

And Aguilar, campesino,
never returned from the trees.

Only Carlos remained.

The last of his troop.

Carlos Fonseca,
bleeding,
alone,
hoping for dawn.

———————

Warm blood seeped
through the hole in his leg.

A steady stream.

Thick and dark.

His tourniquet slid,
lower, lower.

He tied
the soaked rags.

Fingers slipping,
Carlos tied and
re-tied.

But the tourniquet loosened.

The rags slid to knee.

Carlos lay back.

He rested hands
on his chest.

A misted rain fell.

Carlos shivered.

Whispers of steam
rose from his blood.

The moon,
nearly full,

hung at its peak,
lit silver drops
through the trees.

Time stopped,
opened full.

Carlos dreamed
Nicaragua.

———————

Carlos dreamed
five centuries' night.

He dreamed
Black and Red.

Black with greed,
corruption,
empire,
a leaden shadow ever
over the land.

Red with killing
and heat,
mountains melted,
blood in the jungle,
blood in the streets.

The Spanish came first
to enslave.

For the mining
of silver and mercury,
they shipped the
indigenous chained
to Peru.

Then they seized
the best native land
for coffee and cattle.

They forced
the unbroken chain of

slave generations
to build grand haciendas,
to work the plantations,
to sweat, bleed, and die.

The peasants still free
fared little better.

The peasants grew beans and corn
on small plots of land.

The peasant plots
shrank.

The plantations
grew.

Hunger
forced most
into seasonal labor,
peon burdens and debt
few could escape.

Abundant wealth clotted
through the centuries.

Fair-skinned,
land-owning families
seized most of the profits
from fertile Nicaragua.

Those below waited, thirsty,
for trickles.

The great war
of independence
from Spain
changed little for
the peasants and workers.

A new
draining war
quickly followed.

A civil war
between the domestic elites
of Granada and León.

The civil war
lasted decades.

The pendulum crashed
side to side.

Assassinations.

Battles in the field.

Elections at gunpoint
by bribe.

A new empire
descended upon Nicaragua,
greedy as the first.

First,
William Walker

invaded with his mercenary army
to claim the whole nation.

Walker hoped
to take even more,
to reinstate slavery,
to run all the South
like plantation.

But Walker blocked
the ocean-link route of
Cornelius Vanderbilt.

Vanderbilt funded
and armed counter forces.

Walker was defeated,
killed by firing squad.

The North continued
to pressure,
to manipulate,
to control from afar.

When Zelaya's election
threatened profits,
the U.S. invaded,
occupied,
installed Diaz
instead.

Diaz signed over
the railroads and banks.

A line of presidents followed,
meek and corrupt.

Only Augusto Sandino resisted.

The general
and his peasant army
fought the U.S. Marines
for six years.

The U.S., tired,
withdrew.

But,
before leaving,
the Americans
raised and trained
a new force:

The Guardia Nacional.

Led by Somoza.

When Sandino
came to the capital
to negotiate for peace,
the Guardia killed him
in the streets of Managua.

Anastasio Somoza seized power.

The Somoza family dictatorship
would rule Nicaragua for forty-three years.

Nicaragua would suffer
under Anastasio,
then Luis,
then Tachito.

And
Carlos Fonseca
would enter the land
black with their shadow,
red with blood
from Guardia guns.

But Carlos would remember Sandino.

———————

Augustina Fonseca,
the mother of Carlos,
had fled the war zone where
Marines chased Sandino.

She had left
her small mountain village
for the city: Matagalpa.

Young Augustina
found work as a hotel maid.

Earning centavos,
she washed and ironed,
ironed and washed.

She worked long hot days,
year after youth-stripping year.

Carlos,
illegitimate son,
third child of five,
grew up in a home
as small as a closet,
a shed.

Little Carlos,
always hungry,
sold newspapers,
peddled candies
in the street.

The boy,
though poor,

attended school,
learned to read,
devoured books.

The son grew tall like father -
Fausto Amador.

Wealthy Amador,
prodded by his wife,
finally acknowledged
his teen son.

Fausto,
from his mansion,
paid for tuition,
clothes, meals.

Carlos thrived in school.

The wide world opened to his eyes
through history, poetry, literature, science.

And it was Marx that shined most clear.

Marx revealed
the war of classes,
knotted power,
eternal poor.

And Marx gave hope
through workers' rising.

In early writings,
Carlos dreamed of his country,
literate, industrialized, independent, free.

Carlos graduated,
moved to Managua,
worked as librarian.

He rode the bus through the city,
gave books away in poorest barrios,
attended trade and union meetings.

He helped organize
a three-school nationalist march
to a battle site
where invading William Walker
had been repelled.

Carlos moved to León,
began law school.

He joined the defiant student movement,
served as editor of the university newspaper.

Carlos, the young activist,
still believed that unarmed struggle
could topple the dictatorship,
still looked to the Communist Party
for leadership and guidance.

But history's fire would change him.

After the assassination
of Anastasio Somoza
by a young poet in León,
his sons quickly took power:
Luis as president,
Tachito as Guardia head.

Luis declared
a state of siege in León,
blocked the streets with barbed wire,
untied the Guardia leash.

Carlos was among the hundreds arrested.

He spent seven weeks
in a cramped cell,
bodies packed elbows to ribs,
suffocating heat,
one bucket for shit.

Carlos emerged from jail,
sickly, enraged.

———————

When the Cuban Revolution
toppled Batista,
Nicaraguans celebrated
through city and town,
fireworks crackling.

Hearts flared with hope
the Somozas would soon follow.

Carlos and a friend
joined a guerrilla brigade
training in Honduras.

The brigade commander
accepted his friend but
discouraged Carlos.

The commander questioned
Fonseca's resolve.

The commander judged
the thick-glassed law student
too soft for the jungle,
too weak for long marching.

Carlos argued,
persuaded.

After two days in the jungle,
the mosquito-ravaged face of Fonseca ballooned red;
his swollen cheeks nearly buried his eyes.

Carlos marched on.

The commander led his brigade
into ambush.

Six were killed,
fifteen wounded.

Carlos was shot
through left lung.

He lay for weeks
in a prison hospital bed,
vomiting blood,
cheating death.

Carlos questioned,
reflected.

He had learned in the jungle
what no book could teach:

It is the struggle that purifies,
that tests and reveals.

Carlos imagined a new revolution
led by the young,
guerrillas forged by jungle heat,
each a fearless Che Guevara.

A deal was brokered in Honduras,
prisoners deported.

Carlos flew to Cuba,
still bleeding,
on a stretcher.

———————

Cuba welcomed Carlos.

Carlos healed
on the island freed
by Che and Fidel.

News from Nicaragua came.

The Guardia had opened fire
on a protest march of thousands in León;
several students had been killed,
many wounded.

In Cuba,
Carlos found his voice
among the revolutionary exiles
planning their return.

He called their group
the children of Sandino.

The Sandinistas broke
from the slow and tepid
Communist Party.

The Sandinistas set their goals:

Schools before prisons.

Hospitals before barracks.

Freedom from foreign domination.

The land owned
by those who worked it.

The Guardia disarmed.

Old rulers overthrown.

The exiles in Cuba
received a steady stream
of dark reports from their homeland.

More friends and comrades
had been killed in the mountains.

The surviving guerrillas
wandered lost
in small and starving bands.

Carlos braved return
to Nicaragua.

Fonseca was arrested within a month
in the barrios of Managua.

He was badly beaten
in Guardia care.

The officers waited
for the order to
finish their work.

But the student movement exploded
with marches, strikes, and occupations.

Fonseca survived to trial.

He refuted the charges against him.

He accused the dictatorship
of decades-long murder and theft.

He called for
the Nicaraguan young
to take real action,
to abandon the old parties
Liberal,
Conservative, and
Communist.

Convicted,
Carlos served
six months
in prison.

On release,
he was deported.

First,
to Guatemala.

Then,
Mexico.

For long grim years,
the Sandinistas struggled.

Their host of martyrs grew.

Their living ranks drained low
by arrest and disappearance.

The Sandinista leaders in exile
fought to keep their movement
vital and pure.

Carlos argued in letters
against collaboration with
other opposition parties.

He pushed for
higher moral commitment
among cadres,
not greater numbers;
a radical social transformation,
not change of regime;
a focus on the urban underground
and the rural guerrilla,
not farcical elections.

Fonseca braved once more
return to Nicaragua.

He traveled secretly
through the mountains
and jungle of Pancasá.

He walked the dirt paths
village to village,
recruiting peasants for the revolution,
building networks of
safe house and supply.

Fonseca led one of three
guerrilla columns in the region.

He accepted his first women fighters,
defended them against complaints by the men.

Though outnumbered ten to one,
Carlos eluded the Guardia for months.

But the Guardia trapped
the column of Mayorga.

The entire column was wiped out.

The two surviving columns
retreated to Honduras.

The heavy losses in Pancasá
withered Sandinista morale,
caused panic and despair,
sparked fierce debate.

Some argued to continue
the guerrilla war and the
recruiting of peasants.

Others argued for a shift
to political work among students
and the urban poor.

Fonseca
counseled balance,
adaptive fronts,
a hydra revolution.

He saw all work
as vital in the war
against the dictatorship.

From the Cuban example,
he reminded his comrades that
their revolution was still
young and evolving,
their present struggles
the normal pains of growth.

The Sandinistas returned to the fight.

They rebuilt networks
through the mountains.

In the cities,
they organized worker strikes
and protest marches.

They robbed banks
and corporate offices.

They executed
an infamous torturer
of the Guardia.

Fonseca prodded students
to venture out from campus

into factories, barrios,
plantations, villages.

He urged the young
to learn their history,
to step forward and lead.

———————————

The Sandinistas endured
their underground years.

Their leaders,
hunted by the Guardia,
fled safe house to safe house
through the cities.

Carlos lost many comrades,
many friends.

Sotelo shot in the street.

Rugama trapped,
killed.

Buitrago
surrounded by
helicopters and tanks,
shredded.

Other leaders, like Carlos,
suffered long years in prison.

They were hooded, stripped, beaten,
many times tortured and raped.

Carlos exposed
the abuse of political prisoners
to the international press.

Hatred of the
dictatorship grew;
pressure built.

The Nicaraguan young
shouted clear to the world.

Risking freedom and lives,
the students summoned reporters,
occupied campus and cathedral,
marched loud through the streets.

Carlos was freed,
exiled to Cuba once more.

In exile,
Carlos served by word,
not boot and bullet.

He gathered from archives and libraries
the history to be learned by every Sandinista.

The true Sandinista
was the Indian who would not bow
to the Spanish Conquistadores,
the African escaped from
slave ship and plantation.

The people,
the true Nicaraguans,
must not forget
their centuries-deep
tradition of resistance
or their long list
of betrayers.

The great work
begun by Sandino
must be finished.

Sandino,
who could not be bribed.

Sandino,
who could not be beaten.

Sandino,
who fought for Nicaragua
until the Empire fled.

Sandino,
whose work
still remained.

Carlos ached
for his people when
the great earthquake
killed thousands
in Nicaragua.

While the people suffered,
the dictatorship thrived.

The Somozas
siphoned off millions
in international aid.

The poorest earthquake victims
received little help rebuilding,
often none at all.

The Sandinistas seized upon
the rising discontent.

They supported
a wide-spread strike of
construction workers.

They recruited new cadres
across the devastated nation.

They linked with many
sympathizers and collaborators
throughout the worker ranks.

But the growth
led to divisive factions.

Carlos wrote to each
from Cuba.

He prodded
to swifter action
the tendency resigned
to a prolonged struggle,
blind to opportunities,
deaf to workers' voice.

Others,
he reined.

He resisted
the militants planning
arsons and bombings.

He rejected coup plots,
temporary alliances with the
old parties of corruption.

Fonseca argued for
a wiser balance
between political and military work,
a wider outreach
to all types of workers,
a bridging of the networks
between city and village.

Faction leaders inside Nicaragua
resented correction from the exile in Cuba,
challenged his authority.

The factional gulfs only widened
after Sandinista militants
raided a Somocista mansion
and ransomed the guests.

Carlos left Cuba,
returned to his homeland,
hoping to bring
all Sandinistas together.

Carlos passed through safe houses
of the urban underground,
Managua to León.

He planned strategy
with other Sandinista leaders.

He met with sympathizing priests,
Dominicans, Franciscans,
servants unafraid.

Carlos returned
to the mountains and jungle.

He found the situation bleak.

Guerrillas had lived among
the campesinos of remote villages,
shared food and labor,
built a hard-earned trust.

But the Guardia had bombed
and raided the peasant villages,
cut off guerrilla supply lines,
hunted down the small and
fleeing bands.

Slowly, slowly,
Carlos planted seed.

He helped rebuild
the mountain networks:
safe trails,
escape routes,

supply caches,
peasants to be trusted.

He trained the stream of
new recruits to the jungle,
young students from the city.

He tested the recruits
by heavy-laden marches
up and down steep hills,
hard river crossings,
days of burning thirst
and hunger.

When they wanted to quit,
in moments of weakness,
Carlos reminded the recruits that
they were the only hope
of thousands of children,
barefoot, begging,
rag-clothed in the streets.

The mountains
taught discipline,
trust, sharing,
resolve.

The recruits became comrades,
ready to serve.

The strengthening of the guerrillas
did not go unnoticed.

The Guardia launched
a counter-insurgency
with fresh hundreds of troops,
helicopter support,
U.S. advisers.

The Guardia, emboldened,
chased guerrilla bands
deep into the forest.

The Sandinistas lost
old veterans and young recruits,
precious medicine and ammunition,
maps of secret routes.

Carlos led his band
toward the Iyas River.

Pressured on all sides,
outnumbered twenty to one,
Carlos split his band
in four.

He pressed on
toward the river
with Aguilar,
the campesino,
with Carvajal,
the boy.

And the Guardia waited,
ready.

———————

Carlos, shivering,
drew heat from the land,
from miles-deep veins of
melted stone coursing.

He lived to see dawn,
waking land.

The morning breeze
worked through the trees.

Silver leaves flickered.

Carlos smiled,
breathed.

He heard soldiers.

Boots through the mud.

Rising wind.

He saw a pistol raised.

Fired.

But a sudden gust
swallowed the roar.

Then leaves drifted down,
tongues of green,
light as snow.

Through the naked trees,
the sun shined clear.

The star neared the land.

The star
throbbed by
young fire,
glistened pure
with undying white.

Dream of Francis

Peter Bernardone
saved his son from hard labor
in the orchards and fields of Assisi,
from the commoner's small hut,
beds of straw shared with sheep.

Bernardone provided his son
with three years of education,
creeds, psalms, and prayers
learned in Latin.

Bernardone took his son
on long journeys to France,
to merchant fairs bright
with fabric and jewels,
scented with spices,
flowing with wine.

Bernardone apprenticed
his son.

He taught fabric
measures and weights,
bartering, pricing,
all styles of dress
for the rich.

Aggressive, shrewd,
Bernardone thrived in his business.

He bought new lands
outside Assisi,
pastures, orchards,
forests, farms.

Thinly stretched,
Peter trusted young Francis
to steward their shop.

But the father's business bored son.

Francis abandoned his work.

The boy squandered
great wealth with
his friends.

Dressed like princes,
they partied and feasted,
roamed the streets
day and night.

When war with Perugia came,
young Francis and his friends
eagerly joined the men of Assisi.

They rode out to battle,
dreaming of knighthood and glory,
expecting quick work.

But Assisi was crushed.

Her men and boys scattered.

They were hacked down
in vineyards and fields.

———————

The Perugians spared
wealthy Francis.

He was stripped
of fine armor.

He was thrown into prison,
a dark cavernous vault beneath ruins.

Francis entered long night.

Over miserable months,
he learned hunger,
thirst,
biting cold,
choking air.

He heard
the curses and prayers
of men dying.

Francis remembered his old life,
his well-fed days in bright sun,
his nights blurred by wine.

Sweating,
trembling,
malaria fevered,
he remembered starving beggars
he had chased from the shop.

———————

Young Francis languished
a full year in prison.

After his father paid ransom,
Francis suffered another year
ill and bedridden.

Francis recovered,
slowly,
slowly.

Aided by cane,
he rose from his bed.

He walked through the town.

He wandered the streets.

Francis gazed over the land
from a high city terrace.

The land shined with life,
fertile, rich, green.

But the land could not fill
deepest void.

Just as work in the shop,
markets and fairs,
gold coins clinking,
all striving and
hoarding.

Just as hours of gorging,
loud drunken songs,

dizzying wine,
bragging and
strutting.

Though free from prison,
the world felt to Francis
a tightening cage.

He drifted through his days.

Hopeless.

Numb.

———————————

Only a dream of new glory
stirred Francis to life:

A Crusade for Jerusalem.

Knighthoods for the brave.

This would save Francis
from the shop.

This would raise high
with honor.

Leaving Assisi,
Francis encountered an older knight
returning from war.

The knight,
wounded and poor,
crept down the road,
his uniform tattered,
his crest streaked
with blood.

Francis approached
the knight.

He gave up his cloak
in grand gesture.

The knight stared right through him.

Francis traveled south
to Spoleto.

Resting for the night,
his old fever returned.

Delirious,
he dreamed.

God
called him
home.

Back to Assisi.

Francis obeyed.

———————

Francis worked
through the summer.

He worked and
he waited.

All became clear
in San Damiano,
the church of
cracked walls,
rotten beams,
collapsed roof,
wild grass grown
through the floor.

Francis saw light
through the ruin.

He gazed high
to the crucifix
over the altar.

Christ looked down,
warm and kind.

Christ called
his servant
by name.

He tasked with rebuilding.

———

Francis sold everything:
whole bolts of his
father's fine cloth,
his own horse,
his clothes.

Bernadone, enraged,
locked Francis up,
hoping the madness
would pass.

After weeks,
his torn mother
released.

Francis fled
from the city.

He hid in grottos
and caves.

Shivering,
he prayed.

Francis returned to
San Damiano.

He started repairs.

He swept
and he scrubbed.

Bernardone found him,
felt pity.

The father pled
one final time
for his son.

But Francis refused
to go home.

The matter was settled in court,
before the bishop and
all of Assisi.

Naked,
Francis returned
the last of his fine attire.

He gave back
the coins that he owed.

Francis called out to the crowd,
declared that he had no father
but God in Heaven.

———————

The bishop gave Francis
a hermit's tunic and
a traveler's purse.

Francis made pilgrimage
to Rome.

He prayed
in the church
of Saint Peter.

Outside,
he found
a huddle of
sick beggars.

He saw needs
greater than his own.

Feeling sweet freedom,
swept by outpouring love,
Francis gave away every coin
from the traveler's purse.

He rested, alive,
in the hand of the Lord.

———

Wandering north,
Francis came upon a
colony of lepers.

Before,
the merchant's son
had turned away
from the diseased,
wheeled his horse
at their sight.

But now,
he walked among
the blind and the lame,
kissed their hands,
asked forgiveness.

Francis returned to
San Damiano.

He begged alms.

He rebuilt the walls,
stone by stone.

He washed lepers in streams,
rinsed their sores.

———————

When beaten by thieves,
Francis sang.

When pelted by stones,
Francis smiled.

He shared
in the sufferings
of Christ.

Many joined
Francis.

Many healed
by his hand.

Many fed
by the light
in his eyes,
warm and kind,
crystal starlight.

———

Dream of Du Fu

Du Fu came from
a high and privileged clan.

His ancestral veins
throbbed with the blood
of great poets and generals.

A faint maternal line
traced back to the
first emperor of the Tang.

Du Fu, the child,
saw China's full glory,
the peak of the Tang dynasty,
the reign of Xuanzong,
when the granaries overflowed,
when the people walked safe
on all province roads.

In library troves
and orchestra halls,
the child tasted
sweet fruit of the age.

He learned calligraphy art.

He memorized great poems.
of the Han, Sui, and Tang.

By age nine,
the prodigy poured out
his own works,
praised by his teachers.

Of the Phoenix he dreamed,
swirls of red and gold light,
azure feather flames,
the herald of long peace
and blessing.

The child imagined
year after prosperous year,
ever climbing.

By Confucian virtues
- wisdom, honesty, kindness -
his people would thrive.

Young Du Fu
sailed the Yangtze River
toward the sea.

He saw the rich coastal plain,
the burgeoning cities of the delta,
frenetic with commerce and trade.

He stared, awed,
at the harbors alive
with thousands of ships,
the merchant vessel fleets
constantly coming and going,
linking China
to all the vast world.

The Yellow Sea, boundless,
frightened, allured,
sent glistening waves calling
from the isles of Japan.

Du Fu left the coast.

He returned to
his home.

He prepared
for the imperial exam,
the gateway
to all of his dreams.

Du Fu arrived in
the capital, Chang'an,
Eternal Peace.

The city shined
with high culture,
pulsed with life.

Markets teemed
with foreign merchants
displaying the finest goods of
India, Persia, Korea, Japan.

By the imperial palace,
the families of nobility strolled
immaculate gardens,
ornamental lakes,
fruit tree lanes.

The common people made offerings
at temples and shrines,
lit by ten-thousand candles,
scented of flower.

Du learned much from
the calligraphy and painting of Daozi
displayed throughout the capital.

Daozi saw beyond likeness and form.

He captured deep essence
with minimal strokes.

He split lines, scattered dots,
left voids for the mind to fill in.

Each painting was poem.

Du hoped to join Daozi in honor,
his portrait to hang in imperial palace,
his poetry read to the court,
the emperor smiling.

But Du Fu failed
the imperial exam.

Stunned,
he left the capital.

He wandered the land,
seeking roots.

———————————

Du Fu saw Mount Tai,
king of mountains,
his two faces separating
darkness and light,
north and south,
yin and yang.

He wrote of the heights
above bird's boldest wing,
the king's misted breath,
cloud layers falling.

Du sought out
old monks in deep forests.

He learned from masters
of Dao and Zen.

The young poet struggled
to shed will and lose self,
to empty and free.

The unity of Cosmos
eluded.

Presence,
not Absence,
enthralled.

Du Fu found other poets.

They sang to the moon
on spring terraces.

They drank themselves sick.

———————

His traveling ended
with the death of his father.

Honoring tradition,
Du Fu mourned three years
near the family home.

The poet then returned
to the capital.

He took the imperial exam
once more.

Denied position,
blocked by a corrupt high official,
Du Fu made a bold and dangerous appeal
to the emperor himself.

The emperor,
impressed by his writing,
allowed his appointment
to a low-level post.

The first gate had opened.

Du Fu would now serve
the imperial court.

He married
a minister's daughter.

———————

Though wielding little power himself,
Du Fu witnessed all the shifts and turns
of power in highest political circles,
the guile, intrigue, and deception
within the imperial court.

The emperor had aged.

A concubine distracted,
leeched away great wealth.

Officials climbed the ranks
by bribery and deceit.

Frontier wars
drained the granaries.

Taxes soared for the poor.

Du Fu ventured out
from the capital.

He rode through
villages and fields.

The caravans of war
stretched miles,
raised clouds of dust
by war carts' creaking.

Each village yielded conscripts,
their young, their strongest sons.

Old parents leaned and sobbed.

Wives cried out to heaven.

Children stumbled,
clutched at heels.

Back in the capital,
Du Fu was offered promotion.

To district officer.

To judge deserters of the army
and punish draft evaders.

To whip the poor
with unpaid taxes.

Du Fu declined.

Demotion followed.

———————————

Dark times
had just begun
for China and
Du Fu.

In a fearful autumn,
the sky became one cloud;
wind hissed and wailed;
the rain fell, unceasing,
sixty days.

Bog lakes swallowed
half of the capital.

Fungus swept
the grain fields
of the heartland.

The millet rotted black.

Autumn's failed crops
brought cruel winter famine.

The poor sold their blankets
for handfuls of rice;
they shivered and shook
through long nights.

Du Fu sent his wife and children
away from the hunger-stricken capital.

Months later,
he set out to rejoin them.

He passed the imperial palace,
the hot springs where the rich bathed,
donned their silk and sable furs,
listened to fine music,
feasted day and night.

At the separating gate,
he paused,
smelled inside
the wine wasted sour,
good meat allowed to rot.

Outside,
he passed slumped bodies,
the bones of peasants,
frozen,
starved.

Du Fu crossed rivers swollen high,
climbed the mountains north and east.

In the city streets,
old friends and neighbors followed,
heads low,
weeping.

Du Fu had lost his son.

———————

The shadowed land
turned darker still.

After the flood and famine,
China entered civil war.

An Lushan,
the rebel general,
marched his quarter-million men
across the Yellow River.

He defeated imperial forces
at eastern Luoyang,
declared himself emperor.

The rebel army
then marched west
to overthrow Xuanzong.

Terror gripped the capital.

Emperor Xuanzong hesitated,
not knowing who to trust.

Competing factions
split his court.

Though loyal generals held
strong defense lines at Tong Pass,
councillors close to the emperor's ear
stripped the generals of power,
executed all.

Forfeiting advantage,
the imperial army abandoned the pass.

The imperials confronted,
instead,
on the open plain.

The rebels routed,
slaughtered.

Imperial dead
covered the plain,
now a wet-blooded marsh.

Xuanzong deserted his capital,
fled into the northern mountains.

All blame
for the disastrous battle
fell on his concubine
and councillors.

The defeated emperor watched
his foolish advisors killed
by imperial guard,
his beloved mistress
strangled with silk.

—————

Du Fu and his family
joined the panicked hordes
fleeing the capital.

Crimson fire
glowed on their backs as
the temples of the city
burned.

Flaming curtains
wafted through sky,
shriveled black.

Ashes swept
in mournful winds.

The merchant warehouses
vanished in smoke,
vast wealth of the Silk Road
crumbled in embers.

For ten days,
the refugees climbed,
fleeing rebel army.

Winds carried blood
of the plain.

Rains slicked
the steep roads.

Muddy, sodden,
the refugees stumbled,
dragged on.

Roadside,
a prince in tatters
begged food.

But Du Fu
had nothing
to give.

Nothing for strangers.

Nothing for wife,
vacant-eyed,
silent.

Nothing for children,
shaking with hunger,
pleading for sleep,
bitter tears.

————————

They found sweet mercy
in a high mountain village.

They knocked at the gate
of Sun Zai, old friend.

Zai wakened,
welcomed them in.

He lit every lantern.

He brought warm water
for their feet,
hot platters of food.

He drank with Du Fu,
pledged friendship eternal.

Zai shined
bright as moon.

———————

News reached the village.

The emperor had yielded power
to his son, Suzong.

Suzong had stopped running,
turned back.

The Uighurs had promised
to aid the new emperor.

Du Fu left his family
in the northern village.

Duty-bound,
he headed south.

He searched
for the court of Suzong.

But rebels captured Du Fu
in the hills.

His low rank
spared him execution.

He was taken alive,
returned to the capital,
a prisoner and slave.

For a year,
he knew nothing of
his wife and children,
his sister and brothers.

He pulled carts
like a mule in the streets.

Malaria struck,
laid him low.

His captors left him to die.

But Du Fu survived.

Again,
kindness saved.

An abbott welcomed,
embraced.

Du Fu hid
in a monastery cell.

He rested by day,
listened to bells,
the monks chanting
sutras.

The long nights
brought fever and pain.

He paced, sleepless,
through the flickering lamps.

Incense hinted
at mysteries of the earth,
hidden clarity.

Unseen flowers,
first bloom,
promised spring.

Du Fu crafted new poems
as he walked.

A turn of fate.

Aided by mercenaries
Arab, Uighur, and Songdian,
the new emperor reclaimed
the capital.

Imperials found Du Fu
among rebels in the city.

They accused him
of treason.

Du Fu,
eventually freed,
returned to the emperor's court
and resumed his service.

Du Fu pleased
Emperor Suzong.

Suzong promoted,
summoned to his side.

Du Fu scrutinized
official documents,
ensured strict accuracy,
highest style.

But Du Fu stepped too far.

He contradicted the emperor
before the court.

He defended a loyal general
defeated in battle.

Suzong, enraged,
had Du Fu arrested
and tried.

The judges admonished,
but acquitted.

The emperor's anger
cooled over time.

Du Fu was allowed
a short leave.

After a year's separation,
Du Fu reunited with his family
in the northern village.

His son,
shoeless, snow-pale,
clung to his father's knees,
fearful to lose again.

His daughters,
stick-boned,
met him in robes
many times patched
with odd rags.

His wife, speechless,
stared.

Village elders
brought humble gifts:
casks of homemade rice wine,
tasting of dirt.

They asked about
his travels.

They apologized for the wine and
their weed-covered fields:

*Every son
fights the rebels.*

*All work falls on us,
the earth-bent and
crumbling.*

———————

Du Fu returned
to work in the capital.

Again,
he abraded superiors,
refusing to pander or lie.

He was demoted
from the imperial court,
transferred to Huazhou,
buried in paper-mounded
bureaucracy.

He drank to forget.

Aching,
afraid,
he stared at
distant mountains,
deep canyons
rimmed with pine.

New rebel warlords
challenged Emperor Suzong.

The warlords
massacred villages,
raided cities and towns,
killed, raped, and stole
on the open roads.

Chaos clouded the land.

Crops failed.

Again,
the poor starved.

In this dangerous hour,
Du Fu quit his post in Huazhou and
abandoned his official career.

He gathered his family,
yoked his old horse,
packed their cart.

Du Fu followed
in the ancient way,
the path of many
great artist-intellectuals:
the midlife turn from
Confucian ideal of service to state
to the mystical Dao and
the Buddha in nature.

Du Fu, poor,
headed west.

———————

Slowly,
they climbed.

They crept
from pass to pass
through the mountains.

Night and day,
distant war drums,
fearful horns, beacon fires,
prodded them higher.

They forded cold rivers,
crossed icy streams.

They prayed
for their horse
with each slip of hoof,
anguished neigh.

Hungry,
they begged of
lone hermits.

With frostbitten fingers,
they raked frozen turf
for old acorns,
reached through
bramble and thorn
for hard berries.

Winds one day
swept aside the winter mists,

revealed the mountain
shaped like haystack.

Mount Maijishan
dwarfed all other peaks:
a sandstone pyramid,
red, purple, brown,
jutting deep into sky;
with constellations of caves
weaving toward summit
on walls nearly sheer;
with giant Buddhas
carved into cliffs,
gazing down.

In the temple below,
Du Fu found an old friend.

The abbot
who had hidden him
in the capital
helped once again,
welcomed,
embraced.

Exile
had aged
the abbot,
cut deep furrows,
shriveled flesh,
withered skin.

But his eyes held eternity:

The crumbling of mountains.

Valleys' slow rise.

Emptiness forming
to ten-thousand things.

The poet and the monk
talked through the night.

They shared
the full moon.

––––––––––––

Rebel raids
and freezing cold
drove Du Fu south.

Biting gusts
opposed them,
leaden rains,
stinging sleet.

They lost the road,
trackless,
struggled over stone
confusion.

They huddled
midnights
in their cart,
bone to bone,
together shivering,
kept from sleep by
aching hunger.

The children's crying
pierced their father,
each moan and tear
a deeper blade.

Only poetry saved
from madness,
despair.

Du Fu crafted word by word
through the soul-breaking hours
of the night.

Through the day,
his verses carried.

An old man now,
he sang into cold wind
songs of mourning
and lament.

He sang of
his three brothers,
the long roads between them,
separated by armies,
dust of war,
no word or letter
for years;
he envied the cranes
free to fly.

He sang of his sister,
her young husband dead,
children starving,
the swollen river between them
flooded by rage of dragons;
gibbons wail
in dark forest.

Du Fu wondered
who would remember
his songs.

He wondered
what mountain would gather
his bones.

Du Fu pushed on.

And on.

.

———————————

In the night,
they reached a river,
swift, seething,
broad.

A boatman,
for the last of their coins,
ferried across,
laughed through the mist
of high crashing waves.

The little boat lurched,
pitched side to side;
its wooden bones creaked,
near to breaking.

Ashore,
they pressed on
without rest.

They climbed a thin path
growing thinner
and thinner,
a crack through the cliffs,
among clouds.

The path slanted
and veered.

They climbed
gorge after gorge.

Far below,
cascades fell upon stone:
death called clear.

Then, at last,
like a dream crossing dawn,
the Sword Gate appeared.

They passed
through the cliff.

They descended
last hill.

They entered
the plain.

———————————

For a precious
handful of years,
Du Fu found peace
in the plain of Chengdu.

He found
fields tall with grains,
green with rice.

He made friends
in the bustling city.

Gifted some land,
he built a thatched hut
between the river
and woods.

The old poet
turned into farmer.

He gathered herbs,
tended trees of peach and plum,
planted shallots and cabbage.

The clear river flowed
through the idle
spring hours.

Ducklings napped
on the sand, against mother;
kingfishers cried out,
high in bamboo,
magpies danced,
earning mates.

Dragonflies
broke from clouds,
dipped to water,
touched belly tail,
skin of water
unbroken.

Bright flower galaxies
shined on the shore,
young colors
flirting.

Du Fu shared summer wine
with his neighbors and friends.

Under moons full to hollow,
they emptied their jars,
sang like fools,
spit out lees.

But in winter,
the old mountain cold
seized his chest.

Sleepless,
he wheezed
through the night.

He fought
for each breath.

Weary,
he dozed
near to dawn.

Dreaming,
he marched
through the mountains,
marched on and on...

Weary feet.

Grinding bones.

A ghost trapped in night,
cursed to wander.

———————

Peace could not last,
even in Chengdu.

Tibetan forces
drove east.

Rebel warlords
pushed south.

Emperor Suzong,
bedridden, dying,
could not restrain.

The sacred empire
of the Confucian ideal
was no more.

Du Fu,
forced yet again into flight,
resolved to make one final journey.

He planned
to sail the Yangtze
many hundreds of miles.

He planned
to return by land
to his childhood home.

Du Fu set sail.

The great river carried...

Through towering gorges,
carved in deep time,

green-shadowed,
hidden from
sun.

Through narrow-necked rapids,
waters swirling and tossing,
stone echo roar.

Through wide stretches so slow,
boatmen begged help from
the gods of river
and wind.

Du Fu,
still sleepless,
watched moon and stars
through the night.

The waters he rode
taught secrets so clear:

Seasons' wheel.

Rise and fall.

Life by
rivers of water.

Life through
river of stars.

The health of Du Fu,
mid-journey,
turned.

His tired blood
slowed.

His joints swelled
with pain.

Thirsty,
he shook.

Malaria returned.

———————————

Hunger,
sickness, and
ever-flaring war
drove Du Fu from
the Yangtze.

He wandered
Dongting Lake.

He searched for
distant family,
lost friends.

The old man faded
as he searched.

In final winter,
Du Fu furled the sails,
withdrew oars.

He drifted on the lake,
helpless in the wind.

Du Fu remembered.

Young,
he had dreamed
of blinding glory,
leading
the greatest age
of greatest land.

He had gazed
over centuries,

all dynasties past,
certain how bright
he would shine.

But Du Fu had earned
no place in imperial halls,
no admiration of court,
no emperor's praise.

His poems were mere dust
scattered over the land,
dust in the ashes of war.

Du Fu sat
on the boat,
slumped
against mast,
tilted head.

He felt waves
through the wood,
remembered words
of old monk:

*Strength of water
so weak.*

Now he knew.

Night winds pierced,
traveled deep.

Dark clouds
blocked the moon,
hid the stars.

In the old man's
weak eyes,
all was shadow.

But
jade tails
wove
through the
lake depths.

And
wings of azure
coursed
through the
sky.

The waters stilled
with last breath
of Du Fu.

Dragons crossed.

Phoenix carried.

Dream of Becker

Ernest Becker
drew from the depths
of many fields:
cultural anthropology,
post-Freudian psychology,
evolutionary science,
religious studies,
mythology.

Becker explored
the human condition,
the drives and fears of
the Earth-bound
sapien.

The human is first
an organism:
a creature wrapped in skin,
with appendages to move and manipulate,
with a mouth to intake, an anus to expel,
sustained by the consumption
of whole flocks and herds.

Prodded by climate
down from the trees,
the sapiens broke
from other primates.

They walked upright
through the savannah,
hands free, wielding
spears and bows.

They hunted in groups,
developed complex tools,
symbolic language,
diversified roles.

The sapien cortex grew.

Then came
the curse and blessing
of consciousness:
the opening of
Time.

The early humans
saw beyond
the Present moment,
beyond the animals'
eternal now.

The Past opened in their minds
through myth and story,
ancestor legend,
wisdom lore.

And the Future opened too
with hopeful plans,
bright dreams.

But the human
could not fail to see
the dark fate awaiting all.

Each body
would decay.

Each life
would end
in death.

Along among all animals,
the human lived in fear.

————————

Becker believed
Freud had been right
about human anxiety
and repression.

But our deepest
fears and conflicts
were not sexual
in root.

The human feared oblivion:
the pyre, the grave, the tomb,
the swallowing Earth,
the Universe cold.

This was William James'
worm at the core,
the skull grinning in
on our joys.

The human must
build defenses.

The human must
somehow transcend.

Sapiens crossed
continents and oceans.

We built pyramids
like mountains,
towers to the sky.

We waged wars
for kingdoms.

We conquered.

We enslaved.

But still our need burned.

———————

Becker traced
human development
outward from the womb.

The mammal birth was both
miracle and trauma,
a jarring passage
from the safe uterine sea
to the world of light and sound.

The newborn enters helpless,
completely dependent
on the mother
for all nourishment
and ease of pain.

The mother seems like god.

The infant taps her power,
manipulates through
screams and cries.

But the mother often
tires, pulls away,
withholds.

The child feels anxiety,
frustration.

The child learns
to earn comfort, praise, affection;
the parents leverage the child
through stages of growth.

Becker saw paradox,
even tragedy,
in the stages of growth,
each evolutionary gain
coming with steep price.

The inner ego of the child
develops only in reaction
to the outer world.

Intrusion of the Other
precedes concept of the Self.

The Self, unique,
begins as purest imitation.

The child is first a parrot
echoing parents and siblings,
mystified by language
and its symbols.

The child is puppet,
mirroring expressions,
copying postures and movements,
desperate to please.

Ambivalence tears the child.

The ego drives
toward self-mastery,
independence,
control.

But the child,
unable to stand alone,
needs affirming and approval,
the shelter of the group.

The child splits,
creates a hidden
inner world.

The child tells
first lie.

The child likely sees first death
in the animal world -
a bird struck by stone,
broken wings thrashing;
a fish on shore,
gasping gills
fanning slower;
a dog's frozen body
in the field,
eyes without light.

The child feels
terror, dread,
thrill.

The child kills
ants, mice, flies
to feel power.

But death strikes
near to the child,
maybe an uncle or aunt,
grandmother,
grandfather.

The child looks down
in the casket,
sees the bloodless face,
the soulless shell.

The child looks up
at the parents,
no longer sees gods.

Shadow now taints
brightest days.

There is no escape
from the body,
aching, bleeding,
doomed to die.

This truth
would paralyze the
conscious mind;
we cannot bear
the face of death
too close, too clear,
too long.

But the truth, submerged,
can also fuel.

Fear repressed
can drive toward life,
preserve the self,
invigorate,
propel.

Anxiety can raise
to storm subconscious seas,
transmute great tides of energy,
channel for survival.

The child can be saved from oblivion
by society and culture.

The young enter their roles,
earn their esteem,
enjoy status.

Culture provides
purpose and meaning
to the individual life.

Each culture brings
its members together
in a grand performance,
a cosmic drama
where death is transcended,
where heroes live on.

But here again,
a paradox,
a tragedy.

One can enter
the cultural drama
only by submission.

The young must yield to the old.

The young must give themselves over
to the tribe, the state, the elders.

Striving for expansion,
yearning for significance,
hoping for immortality,
the lone life shrinks
into the crowd.

———

Becker saw transference
in this exchange.

The human born helpless
is overwhelmed by the world,
a dwarf among giants,
a speck among stars.

No one can take in
the outrageous power,
the fearful chaos
of the universe.

So the child transfers
all awe and terror
from the vast beyond
to a single face.

The child attempts
to combat, control, appease
the object of transference.

But the child
seeking freedom
is now bound,
dependent on the object,
still insecure,
small.

Becker viewed transference
as a necessary tool for survival.

Growth can be traced
by the widening range of

transference objects
as the human ventures
deeper into life,
further in the world.

From parents.

To teachers.

To superiors.

To rulers.

Becker saw great danger
if transference stopped
short of the Cosmic Power,
endowing only emperors
and kings.

———————

Becker searched for
the roots of inequality
and war.

He delved
into the primitive mind
through the work of
Hocart, Rank, and Brown.

The primitive,
intimate with nature,
sought the power of the sun,
source of all life.

The primitive wondered
at the mysteries of the earth,
how tiny seeds buried,
sprinkled with rain,
turned to forests,
gardens.

Through dances and chants,
the primitive dramatized
the great forces of nature.

Through communal rituals,
the primitive promoted fertility
of the land and the womb.

In the early sapien tribes,
each member could participate
in the regeneration of life,
each could feel a part of
cosmic creation.

Though the early hunters
shared their kills,
all were not equally esteemed
within the tribe.

Some were admired for skill
in dancing, singing, storytelling;
some stood out by dexterity,
strength, handsome face.

These traits and abilities alone,
though advantageous,
made few chiefs.

The people looked more
to the hero.

The stoic warrior
daring raids on the enemy,
leading hunts of huge prey.

The scarred killer
adorned with trophies:
scalps, feathers, claws.

The hero who defied death.

The hero who claimed the
life force of others.

The hero,
a shield against fear.

———————

Becker traced forward
from the primitive mind
to the ancient.

With agricultural surplus
and the rise of cities,
kings replaced
chiefs.

The king derived his power
from mystification
as much as crude force.

Sacred rituals
performed by temple priests
confirmed the deity of the king,
his divine right to rule.

The king in
poetry, myth, painting
shined like the sun
on his people,
shared in the
light of the gods.

And the king,
by right, seized
sons for his army,
daughters for concubines,
the best fields of the land.

Men hoped
for a small share
of his glory.

At least they could rule
their own homes.

———————————

The people served
Pharoahs, Caesars, Sultans, Khans.

The people built
palaces and castles,
bridges, gates, and walls,
monuments and statues -
all signs of blessing
from the gods.

And the rulers amassed gold.

Sacred gold,
symbol of immortal sun.

Enduring gold,
never rusting,
never aging.

The first banks and mints
were temples.

Early priests trafficked
in golden amulets and charms.

The priests received
first fruits, choice meat;
by sacrifice and prayer,
they interceded for the poor.

First gods,
then kings,
then presidents

gazed eternal
on our coins.

In the modern sapien,
Becker saw a creature
still denying,
still enslaved.

So confident in reason,
the modern human looked down upon
the ancients and their superstitions.

So proud of industry and science,
the modern sneered at
primitives naive with life force symbols,
engrossed in spirit worlds.

But our progress came
with a price.

In severing
from the supernatural,
we left ourselves only
the material world
to claim:
the Earth would bear
all our vicious striving.

Imperial nations warred,
swept continent and sea,
laid railroad tracks,
paved roads.

We cleared forests
for our cities,
drained our lodes

and mines,
drilled for gas
and oil.

Our factories churned out
engines, motors,
airplanes,
cars.

Smoke poured into sky.

Toxins settled
in our soil.

Poisons spread in
oceans, rivers, lakes.

The planet warmed.

———————

Though the modern sapien
held no gold in hand,
money still meant power.

The modern craved power
as much as the primitive,
the ancient.

And the only power
worth seeking was
ultimate power,
power to shine,
power to last.

Money could stretch life
by best medical care.

Money could grow,
properties pass within family,
dynasties endure by inheritance.

Money could commission portraits,
start foundations and trusts,
name airports and towers,
freeze bodies someday
to be raised.

What could the poor,
the common worker,
feel but envy?
diminishment in shadow?

Modern culture
-materialist, capitalist, consumer-

set the value of a life
by bank balance,
size of house,
speed of car.

The worker,
feeling small,
trusted culture to relieve.

The worker labored.

The worker strived.

But few could reach the top.

The worker numbed,
distracted.

The worker looked at those below,
found hollow satisfaction.

And here was
inequality's dark root.

———————

Becker saw
the root of war
as intertwined.

Leaders rise,
rally the discontented,
promise a nation
unique in the world,
immortal in history.

Followers swell
with the hope of prosperity,
a golden age dawning.

But the gathering banner
also excludes.

Those not marching beside
become enemies,
obstacles to progress,
opponents to be purged.

The leader projects
the people's fears and frustrations
outside of their circle,
demonizes the foreigner,
the immigrant,
the stranger.

The leader flexes power
through the streets
by torch,
by club,

by gun.

The leader wages war.

Not a war of aggression.

A sacred war.

Crusade.

To remove the tainted.

To bring the golden age.

———————

Becker saw symbiosis
in the relationship between
followers and leader.

The leader,
radiant, magnetic,
gains the adulation
of the throng.

The leader basks
and feeds.

But the leader
must provide a
time-transcending vision,
must compel by
blinding myth.

Only myth and vision
can unify
a chosen people,
a motherland,
a fatherland,
a revolution.

Only a pure
and sacred struggle
can raise the people
to heroics.

For this they will die.

For this they will kill.

The sanctified war grants immunity.

———————————

To Becker,
all came back
to animal fear and
denial of death.

An aura of invincibility
wrapped the leader.

So confident
the leader spoke,
so stoic and sure
the orders of execution.

We felt like children again,
safe and secure,
protected by parents'
omnipotent shield.

We shared in the power.

We released
our shadow selves
upon the scapegoat,
freed hidden impulses,
secret wishes.

We lived through our leader.

Behind our guns,
we, too, became
masters of fate,
watched our prisoners
tremble.

———————

Ernest,
battling cancer,
facing his own end,
drove still deeper,
ever deeper,
into truth.

There was hope
for humanity.

We could shed
our illusions.

We could admit
our creatureliness,
embrace our kinship
with animals.

We could raise our eyes
to the starry threads of
vast cosmic web.

We could transfer
our terror and awe
to Creator.

Each small life
could pour out
into Nature,
humbly expand,
meekly endure,
join the great
cycles and tides.

———————

Ernest Becker,
young Jewish soldier,
had helped liberate
a death camp.

He had seen the dead
piled, tossed, burned:
work of the Nazis.

Ernest, haunted,
spent the rest of his life
searching for answers.

Few have delved
so deeply into science and art.

Few have faced
so bravely the grim answers
that he found.

Even as the cancer spread,
crippled, stole his last strength,
Ernest sought truth.

He learned
how the dying seed lives,
how light soar the free.

His work waits to guide
every seeker.

———————

Waking

We wake from our dreaming.

We know who we are.

———————

We accept the hard truth:

There will be no return
to the Earth.

———————————

We must stay alive.

We must find new worlds.

All we have
is each other.

———————

We pass a dead probe,
eons old,
charred by the rays
of deep space.

We near a young star.

A gas-giant planet.

An icy-poled moon
thawed at equator,
crack-veined with
blooms of green algae.

WELLSPRINGS

<u>Saigyō</u>

Gazing at the Moon:
Buddhist Poems of Solitude
Meredith McKinney

Awesome Nightfall:
The Life and Times of Saigyō
William R LaFleur

<u>Kafka</u>

The Trial

Metamorphosis

The Hunger Artist

In the Penal Colony

Before the Law

Amerika

<u>Black Elk</u>

Black Elk Speaks
John G Neihardt
www.bisonbooks.com

Nicholas Black Elk:
Medicine Man, Missionary, Mystic
Michael F Steltenkamp

The Sixth Grandfather:
Black Elk's Teachings Given
to John G Neihardt
Edited by Raymond J DeMallie

———————

Sinéad O'Connor

This Is A Rebel Song

I Am Stretched On Your Grave

He Moved Through the Fair

Black Boys on Mopeds

Three Babies

Silent Night

<u>Kathë Kollwitz</u>

Mother With Dead Child

The Downtrodden

The Volunteers

The Survivors

March of the Weavers

From Many Wounds You Bleed,
O People

Never Again War

The People

Uprising

Outbreak

Need

———————

<u>Carlos Fonseca</u>

Sandinista:
Carlos Fonseca and
the Nicaraguan Revolution
Matilde Zimmermann

Sandinistas:
A Moral History
Robert J Sierakowski

Carlos, the Dawn is No Longer Beyond Our Reach:
Prison Journals of Tomas Borge

Sandino's Daughters:
Testimonies of Nicaraguan Women in Struggle
Margaret Randall

Open Veins of Latin America:
Five Centuries of the Pillage of a Continent
Eduardo Galeano

Born in Blood and Fire:
A Concise History of Latin America
John Charles Chasteen

William Walker's Wars
Scott Martelle

<u>Saint Francis</u>

The Complete Francis of Assisi:
His Life, the Complete Writings, and 'The Little Flowers'
Jon M Sweeney

Reluctant Saint:
The Life of Francis of Assisi
Donald Spoto

Richard Rohr

<u>Du Fu</u>

Du Fu:
A Life in Poetry
David Young

The Selected Poems of Tu Fu
David Hinton

China's Greatest Poet:
In the Footsteps of Du Fu
Michael Wood

Ernest Becker

The Denial of Death

Escape From Evil

*The Birth and Death
of Meaning*

———————

LOVE AND THANKS

Heather

Mom and Dad

Allen and Rhonda

Reid Gerken

Scott Mitchell

Dustin Riedel

Jennifer Chikhani

Luke Danz

Jon Welge

Dawn Ruskan

<u>Also by Gary David Springer</u>

Toshiro Burning

Caravaggio's Crossing

Fire of Life

Phera

Gabriel

Fuegos

Coma Dreams

<u>Contact</u>

gary_springer@hotmail.com